Fox wandered past a deep well of water.
She stared down and admired her
bright coat.

Fox leaned so far over that she slipped!

Splash! Fox landed in the water.

She clung to the rocky sides.
"I will never escape!" she whimpered.
Along came Goat and peered into the well.

Her mighty horns blocked the sun. "Whatever are you doing down there?" she asked.

Fox stopped whimpering, and smiled.
"Why Goat," she said, "haven't you heard?"
"Heard what?" asked Goat.

"A long hot drought is coming.
The grass will wither. The streams will dry up.

You will be hungry and thirsty."

Goat looked worried.
"But you haven't answered my question," she
said. "Why are you down the well?"

"When the hot drought comes, I will be cool," Fox said. She grinned slyly at Goat and added, "I will have plenty of water to drink."

Goat said, "That sounds good!"
"You should join me," said Fox.
Quick as a wink, Goat sprang down the well.

Splash! She landed by Fox.

Quick as a second wink, Fox jumped onto
Goat's high horns.
From there, Fox sprang out of the well.

"Now I am stuck alone down here!" cried Goat. Fox laughed. "You should have looked before you leaped."

Goat waited a long time to be rescued.
At last a boy threw her a rope and pulled
her out.

Goat thanked him and said,
"Next time, I will think about things before
I do them."